ABER TIDY

by Brian Radford

Published by New Generation Publishing in 2018

First Edition

www.newgeneration-publishing.com

New Generation Publishing

WELCOME
to Aber Tidy,
a town in
Doolally Valley,
somewhere
in Wales...

FOR a whole year, I witnessed incredible events in Aber Tidy, a one-time mining town in Doolally Valley, that left me gasping in disbelief.

Many times my sides ached for days from laughing at the ludicrous things that were said and done in this incomparable community.

Forever, I will cherish the outrageous fun, chilling drama, explosive personal clashes, and the rugby club that became the first in the world to sign a hooker from the Red Light district.

What impressed me most was the natural wit, and insatiable appetite for a rattling good giggle.

Should you ever feel sad or low, I strongly recommend a week in the classy Bell Hotel – fabulous food, and luxury beds - and laugh yourself to sleep.

And do make sure you are well stocked with a large box of soft tissues to mop up the tears.

One day, I will go back. It's unique, and irresistible. I'm already looking forward to it.

Reporter: Brian Radford

A massive 'thank you' to art student Faye Deacon – alias Peggy Pastel – for her imaginative sketches that depict a series of dramatic events in the incomparable Aber Tidy.

DIOLCH YN FAWR

JANUARY

'Butterfingers' is left holding the baby!

FORMER head teacher Mansel Thomas, chairman of Aber Tidy town council, wished his colleagues 'good luck' for the coming year, and especially to the struggling football club that had lost every match of the season so far, and conceded a League record of 127 goals in just five months.

Councillor Thomas singled out luckless goalkeeper 'Butterfingers' Jenkins, who had also dropped 29 catches in 20 matches as wicket-keeper for the cricket club last summer.

Mr. Thomas' voice dropped sharply as he expressed "profound concern" that Mr. Jenkins had just been appointed a senior assistant at the Maternity Clinic.

There he would be part of a team that demanded safe hands to take new-born babies from their mums, and then put them down gently in a nearby cot.

Mr. Thomas said that every councillor should consider the “seriousness of the situation”, and he urged them to say a short prayer for all the babies who would be picked up by ‘Butterfingers’, asking that he should hold on to them safely at all times.

+++++++++++

LATER in the month Katy Morris, plain Katy Klepto to the police, was caught stealing a tin of peaches in Tesco supermarket.

In court, Justice Wigmore said he would be sending her to jail for a month for every slice in the tin.

There was sudden uproar in the public gallery where her husband, Idwal, had leapt to his feet, and called out, “That woman is my wife, and she also stole a large tin of garden peas!”

+++++++++++

PROPERTY builder Bill Kitchen has quit Labour and joined the Conservatories.

+++++++++++

BERYL Rees would only eat organic fruit, and she sent her husband, Bert, to Aber Tidy vegetable market where he stopped at Mike Brown’s stall, and said: “These apples and pears are for my wife, have they been sprayed with any of that poisonous stuff?”

“Definitely not,” said Mike. “You’ll have to do that yourself!”

+++++++++++

FATHER of 12, Dick Long, finally decided on a vasectomy, and said it was a ‘snip’ at £20!

+++++++++++

POLICE and the RSPCA launched a thorough search of Aber Tidy's popular pet shop after the owner was heard to say, "See you later, alligator!"

+++++++++++

WHEN Dai Twp (stupid) Richards had a plastic hip replacement, he asked the surgeon if he could take the bone home for his dog.

"I'll do better than that," said the surgeon, "I'll let you have every bone after every operation."

"Oh, thank you very much," said Dai.

"Matron's right, you are bone idol!"

+++++++++++

ENGINEER George Evans returned to Aber Tidy late one night after three months working on a ship at sea.

His legs were like jelly, as he speedily zig-zagged along the pitch-black High Street, caused by the Fiddler family who, yet again, had plugged into the main electricity supply, and used up all the power.

In the dark, trainee police officer Ron Howells thought George was a motor-bike with a quiet engine, and when it refused to stop, he booked it for not having a back light!

+++++++++++

TEENAGER Peggy Jones emerged as a potential professional artist after misreading a council advertisement in The Gazette.

Councillors were desperate not to repeat last year's poor carnival sponsorship, which had plunged to an all-time low.

The bold advertisement urged "draw a crowd to boost carnival income."

And Peggy did just that!

Using her vast HB kit, she literally drew a carnival scene with the young queen sitting on the back of a lorry, surrounded by traditional bunting, balloons, and flags of virtually every nation.

As the year went on, she became plain Peggy Pastel, producing a continuous flow of sketches to record the main events in the valley.

+++++++++++

WHEN lightning lit up the golf course, Dai 'twp' Richards thought it was someone taking photographs.

And when the rain teemed down, he sheltered under a big oak tree, and couldn't understand why everyone was running past him to the clubhouse, especially as the 'flash-bulbs' were still going off.

+++++++++++

HORACE Roberts, married with five children, admitted that he was having sex on the side. Left side to be precise!

FEBRUARY

Amazing Welsh wizard shocks quiz duo!

DEEP in the woods in Doolally Valley lives the incredible Welsh wizard – not the three bears – who has the world's greatest memory.

He has white, shoulder-length hair, a long, goatee beard, and can answer the trickiest questions on sports events with astonishing accuracy.

Edith Allen's 18-year-old son, Stephen, and his mate, Stuart Atkinson, decided to visit the Welsh wizard to test him with an absolute corker.

After walking for an hour, the lads finally found the wizard sitting outside his crumbling cabin, puffing a pipe, and reading the Western Mail.

"Good afternoon, sir," said Stephen.

"We understand that you can recall the result of any major football match played in Wales since 1950, and we'd like to see if that's true, if that's all right with you."

The wizard nodded, and held his hands out to indicate that he was ready for Stephen to put his question.

"Right," said Stephen, "can you tell us the final score

between Newport County and Gillingham in October 1950, and who scored the goals, if any goals were scored?"

The wizard nodded to confirm he understood the question, and said, with a definite Port Talbot tongue, "Newport County one-nil. Shergold scored the goal, and the attendance was 9828."

Stephen and Stuart were stunned. He was spot on. They thanked him, and went on their way, mystified.

Then, a few weeks later, Stephen suggested to Stuart that they should go back for another chat with the amazing wizard.

And as they approached him, Stuart raised his hand in a friendly gesture, and said "How!" – short for 'howdy' - and in a flash, the wizard replied, "Close-range volley!"

+++++++++++

BAPTIST minister Gary Roberts was fined £100 for parking his car on the pavement close to his chapel's front door.

In mitigation, he told Justice Wigmore that the man who sold him the car was adamant that it would need at least one service a year, and that this was the closest he could get!

+++++++++++

A council lorry overturned on an icy patch of road near the Aber Tidy roundabout.

Police officers approached a man sitting at the roadside with his head in his hands, and pointed to the vehicle.

The man looked up, and said, "No, that's not mine. My lorry doesn't have wheels on the top!"

+++++++++++++

URINALS have been raised in the Aber Tidy racecourse weighing-room to keep jockeys on their toes!

+++++++++++++

TWO masked men raided Don Patel's corner shop and drove off with 3,000 cigarettes.

When asked if he'd recognize them again, Don replied, "For sure, they were Benson and Hedges!"

+++++++++++

BETHEL'S dodgy treasurer Bill Greenhill returned to Scotland after being sacked for fiddling chapel funds.

With a twinkle in his eye, the minister, Dewi Joseph, began his next service… "Our opening hymn today is number 534, There is a Green Hill far Away…"

+++++++++++

BUTCHER'S assistant, George Pork, has been given the chop!

+++++++++++

WIND-UP specialist Roger Miller went into Tesco and said to the shy assistant, "What's someone like you doing here? You're beautiful. You should be in Hollywood."

Flattered and blushing, she said, "Thank you so much. You're so kind."

Then Roger's brother, Mark, chipped in, "Tell her you've lost your lenses, and you're on your way to Specsavers!"

MARCH

Helicopter ejector seat a 'no brainer!'

ABER Tidy town council rejected a Doolally Valley company's request to fit ejector seats on helicopters after the spinning blades had decapitated a plastic dummy on a test run.

Councillor Joe Grierson called it a "no brainer!"

+++++++++++

AS ghost stories go, the one involving the Lewis family, of Butterscotch Crescent, is an absolute classic.

The town council built all 30 houses in this close-knit community way back in the Fifties.

Jack and Mary Lewis, along with their four children, lived in number 13, opposite the bus stop.

Shortly after they moved in Tom, eldest of the four, and a week from his 12th birthday, told his parents that he kept hearing voices, shouting 'Help! Help! Fire ! Fire!' in his bedroom.

The voices came from behind the wall alongside his

bed, which scared him, and he refused to sleep there again.

So Jack and Mary then slept in the room, and they, too, were disturbed by the voices Tom had heard.

They also noticed that the street lamp outside their house was the only one of 30 in the crescent that was not working.

Jack reported the broken street lamp to the council, but its most senior engineer failed to find anything wrong, and went away baffled.

"Very odd," he said. "Maybe, it's a ghost that's up to no good."

Jack froze on the spot. He couldn't dare tell him about the bedroom voices, or he really would think the place was haunted.

Instead, he asked Father Brown, of St. Joseph's, if he would call and exorcise every room to drive out any demons.

Father Brown spent ten minutes in each room, determined to remove everything that was evil.

Sadly, his immense effort didn't work and, according to the Lewis family, the voices continued to be there, though not every night.

Some council bosses cynically thought the Lewis family had invented the 'ghost' to get a bigger and better house.

Jack then remembered a similar 'haunted house" mystery in North London in summer 1977.

The Hodgson family reported that tables and chairs were moving on their own, crockery was hurtling through the air, and there were knocking noises, and an elderly man mumbling in their Enfield home.

A highly respected psychic researcher launched an investigation, and was struck on the head by a flying Lego block while alone in the kitchen.

The Enfield mystery was never solved, and doubters again thought that the family could be using tricks to fool the council into giving them a larger house.

Jack then spent a day at the library perusing archive

editions of The Gazette, desperately hoping to find a report of an incident back in time on the ground where his house now stood.

And he was just about to give up and go home when, staring him in the face was the big, bold headline---'Pensioner Dies in Aber Tidy House Blaze.'

And he read to himself… "A pensioner died in a fire at his home in Aber Tidy earlier this week.

"He was asleep in his bed when the fire broke out at around 2.00 a.m. in Butterscotch Crescent…"

Jack headed straight to the council's morose housing manager who, on this crucial information, reluctantly accepted that the house could, indeed, be haunted, and he agreed to move the Lewis family to a brand new, three-bedroom property in Islwyn Evans Drive.

Workmen boarded up Number 13, and the council announced that it would never be lived in again.

Yet, the biggest mystery of all came just two nights after the Lewis family had left when the street lamp was suddenly shining again…

+++++++++++

BOXING champion Charlie Harris was arrested while breaking into Beynon's furniture store, taking back a kitchen table with long and short legs.

+++++++++++

EVERY school in Aber Tidy celebrated Saint David's Day on the first morning of the month.

Boys were turned out in pristine white shirts, scarlet waistcoats, red bow ties, and dark trousers, while the girls wore the national costume of red jacket, red dress, black-and-white pinafore, and black funnel hats, and there were enough daffodils and leeks to open a market stall.

Joe Bevan's parents got confused, and thought it was Christmas Day, and dressed him up as a reindeer.

+++++++++++

PET shop owner Brian Nobes stressed that he had never sold a wasp, and that the two in the window were on death row.

+++++++++++

PHOTOGRAPHER Keith Scanner amazingly escaped injury when his studio collapsed after Janet Evans had asked for her wedding pictures to be blown up.

+++++++++++

THE incredible John 'Rambo' Phillips continues to have sex at 85, and live at 74!

+++++++++++

OUTSIDER Super Cat won the Aber Tidy Grand National by a whisker! Hot favourite, Lord Sinus, didn't get a sniff!

+++++++++++

GARDENING guru Tony Thorp stressed that the vacancy in his fencing team was for an experienced panel fitter, not an Olympic swordsman.

+++++++++++

DAI 'twp' Richards volunteered for weekend work at the fireworks factory where he hoped to meet Catherine Wheel.

He said, "I've heard that she's really spectacular at night. Definitely my type!"

Dai also began part-time work at the broken biscuit repair factory, and said, "I'm putting fractured chocolate fingers into splints.

"Must say, our boss, Jacob, is a cracker!"

++++++++++++

POSTMISTRESS Alice Stamp's 17-year-old son, Mike, telephoned from Newmarket, where he's training to be a jockey, to say he'd put on a stone, and grown a foot, so she sent him an extra sock!

++++++++++++

CANOE champions Pete and Di drifted into the shipping lane in front of a Japanese tanker.

Captain Kawasaki Yamaha, using a megaphone, raged: "Me captain on Bridge, you silly assos. You damage ship, and me sue."

Water was seeping into Pete's frail craft, Kiwee Too, from high waves caused by the tanker.

Responding to Pete's desperate plea for help, Lifeboat headquarters asked: "What is your position, sir?"

"Managing-director," Pete replied. "But not for long if you don't get a move on!"

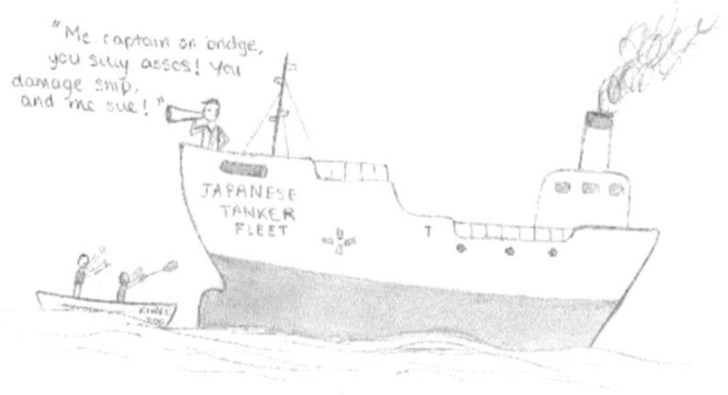

APRIL

Bus users furious at 'stops being pulled out'

ELDERLY residents, who rely on the local bus service for their weekly trip to the shops, were furious when Prime Minister, Theresa May, said she'd be 'pulling out all the stops' to make Brexit work.

+++++++++++

DOCTOR Morgan Owen invited Bob Parry to his surgery when told that the 92-year-old retired solicitor was about to marry stunning Elsie Davies, the 25-year-old carnival queen.

Dr. Owen told Bob that, because of his age, he should consider having a full-time lodger to help with the chores.

He quickly decided on Elsie's 27-year-old cousin, Mary, another blonde stunner.

Now, a year later, Dr. Owen rang Bob to find out how well married life was going for him.

Bob said, cheerfully: "It's awesome! We have a wonderful baby boy!"

Shocked, but impressed, Dr. Owen asked, “And what about Mary, your lodger?”

“Oh, she’s got one, as well!”

+++++++++++

ABER Tidy rugby club made history when they signed a high-class hooker from Red Light Rovers.

With her blazing auburn hair, bent nose, cauliflower ear, and thighs like tree trunks, fearsome Freda Phipps vowed to make it her business to scare the pants off everyone who faced her in the scrum.

And she had hands as big as spades to grab whatever swung her way!

+++++++++++

PAUL and Becky were poised to take their marriage vows at St. Mary’s church when chaos broke out.

They were literally set to exchange wedding rings when the Rev. Bryn Williams told the packed congregation that if anyone had good reason to object to their becoming man and wife to declare it there and then.

And a voice boomed high in the rafters, “One, two, three, testing! Three, two, one, testing!”

Paul buckled at the knees, and fell into the minister’s arms. It was just as well it wasn’t ‘Butterfingers’ Jenkins, or he would have crashed to the floor.

A paramedic rushed from the congregation and fetched a glass of water, and a chair for Paul to sit on.

Time was then allowed for Paul to regain composure, though he stayed in the chair for the rest of the service.

It was only when Becky and groggy Paul were walking down the aisle that a head was seen peeping over the balcony rail.

The couple’s photographer had climbed to the highest point in the church to take a heavenly picture, and tripped over a heap of wires, and set off the recording equipment…

+++++++++++

THE Football Association surprisingly granted Aber Tidy FC permission to close the gates on its supporters---to keep them INSIDE the ground until the match was over.

Supporters' Club chairman, Andy Lloyd, 79, joked: "We've been studying old black-and-white films of prisoners escaping from detention camps, and been impressed by how they dug tunnels to get out.

"Most of us are in our seventies, but we've all got shovels…"

+++++++++++

TWO long-term prisoners have turned down the chance of an early release from their 30-year sentence because a compulsory parole condition is to watch three matches of the Aber Tidy football team.

Tommy 'animal' Lewis stormed, "I've served 20 years for a double murder. I've paid the price.

"Being asked to watch Aber Tidy football team is a step too far. The punishment doesn't fit the crime."

+++++++++++

COMPULSIVE gambler Llew Morgan lost £50 on a horserace, and a further £50 on the TV replay!

+++++++++++

ITALIAN ice-cream seller, Luigi Vanilla, has joined the cornet section of the Aber Tidy Silver Band.

+++++++++++

'GUESS the Dad' was launched after spinster Blodwen 'battleaxe' Morris let slip that she had two secret sons, both under 12.

Blodwen dropped the bombshell when taking six

children to school in her 4 x 4, and a police officer called out from his car, “Stop! Stop! You must stop!”

“But only two are mine!” she shouted back, prompting the biggest guessing game in Aber Tidy history.

Large posters started to appear in the town, dramatically asking, ‘Who is the Daddy of them All?’

Worried wives and partners demanded DNA tests to get quick and conclusive answers.

The Battered Husbands’ First Aid centre was urgently reopened after The Gazette reported a rush on baseball bats.

Frosty Blodwen refused to leave her home as hostile wives were waiting outside to grill her—verbally for sure, and physically on the barbecue, if she didn’t reveal names.

It had always been thought that Blodwen’s sister, Vera, was mother to the lads, while they all lived happily together in Donkey Street.

Bookie Ben Wright offered odds on the likely dad, with 92-year-old Bob Parry, the indefatigable Valley stallion, the inevitable hot favourite.

Tension grew, and gossip escalated, as the DNA results were expected in the next 24 hours.

+++++++++++

ACCOUNTANT Max Avoidance was in the Royal Oak figuring out how to murder his wife when best mate Arthur walked in.

Max told Arthur – known to friends as Arti – that he was looking for someone to get rid of his wife so that he, as next in line, could claim her insurance cover.

“Don’t fret,” said Arti, “I’ll do it for you. And for just 25p! We’ve been mates a long time.”

Max then revealed his chilling plan, telling Arti that his wife went to the Tesco store at 10.30 every Tuesday morning, wearing an ankle-length white raincoat, and a bright red scarf.

“Simple,” said Arti, “you just leave it to me.”

While Arti waited at 10.30 on the next Tuesday morning, a tall woman, wearing a long, white raincoat, and a red scarf, walked into the store right on time.

Arti followed her to the quiet bakery area, strangled her, and dropped her down among the pile of empty cardboard boxes.

"Easiest 25p that I've ever picked up," he muttered.

But then, just as he was about to leave the store, another woman, also dressed in a long, white raincoat, and wearing a bright red scarf, was striding towards him.

"Can't take the chance," he thought, and again followed her to the bakery corner, strangled her, and left her alongside his earlier victim.

However, this time, the store's wide-eyed security officer caught him in the act, and called the police, who told The Gazette, who headlined the story, 'Arti chokes two for 50p at Tesco!'

+++++++++++

HANNAH Gutteridge was cooking a full English breakfast when she answered the doorbell.

On the step was strapping Danny Hughes, the toughest double-glazing salesman in the whole of Wales.

The champion. The one that even the meanest Scot found impossible to turn down.

Hannah charmingly steered him to the softest seat in the lounge, handed him a steaming cup of coffee, and put his large, black briefcase alongside the piano, while she returned to the kitchen.

Minutes later, she said, "Come and join me. You've got two eggs, bacon, beans, mushrooms, tomatoes, and two slices of toast."

Danny was flabbergasted. Then they ate together, and Hannah asked him," So why are you here?"

In deep shock, he replied, "I've no idea. Nothing has happened to me like this before." And the baffled champion wandered off, leaving his briefcase alongside the piano…

+++++++++++

SCHOOL prefect Stan Ball fell off his bike in Rimmer Street, and was lying in the gutter when a police officer asked him for his name to tell his parents.

Stan looked up, and said: "But my parents know my name!"

+++++++++++

STARGAZERS at Aber Tidy's popular Stellar Club were thrilled with their new telescope. Some even thought that it had located an unknown planet.

Club chairman Jim Willson announced the discovery at an astronomers' conference in Cardiff.

Several international experts then travelled to Aber Tidy to look into the telescope to see the 'planet' in close-up.

Dai 'twp' Richards, a club member for 20 years, said his friend, Andy, had been to Mars, and had met the Martians, who gave him lots of chocolate bars, and were normal people.

Dai said that Andy went to Mars in Slough, and got there by train, and didn't need a rocket from NASA in the United States.

Andy became known as '18 months' after a slate fell off a roof and sliced away part of his left ear, which left him with a (y) ear and a half, in other words 18 months!

A professor from Beijing was the first to express doubts on it being a planet, and asked to take a closer look.

A fire engine was brought alongside the telescope so that the professor could climb its ladder and examine the lens.

Very quickly a smile crossed his usually inscrutable face, as he reached out and pulled a piece of paper off the lens---the assumed planet.

He handed it to chairman, Jim Willson, who said: "Sadly, we have nothing to celebrate. It was this…"

He held up the piece of paper, and said: "I will read what it says… 'Tesco's finest steak and kidney p…'"

It then emerged that Dai 'twp' Richards had just eaten his ready-made lunch before starting to assemble the telescope, and that part of the packet had become stuck to the lens.

So what they thought was a fascinating new planet, was simply pie in the sky!

+++++++++++

CALENDAR factory boss has sacked Tal Joseph for taking a day off!

+++++++++++

BUS driver Billy Williams had problems with his root, and was in agony when he entered the new dental practice in Molar Road.

Billy admitted to young dentist, Phil Cavity, that it was his first extraction, which made him extremely nervous.

Billy was leaning back in the chair, his mouth wide open, when he saw, out of the corner of his eye, Dr Cavity approaching with a needle shaking violently in his hand.

"Must be honest," said Dr Cavity, "I know exactly how you feel, it's my first extraction, as well!"

MAY

A load of bull from the local spy!

EVERY day without fail, Martha Bowen sits in her Gooseberry Street front room, and gently pulls back the curtain and peeps out to see what is happening.

One afternoon she saw the farmer's daughter, a lovely young lady, with long golden hair, leading a cow to a bull at a nearby farm.

Martha dashed into the street, and said to the beautiful young lady, "Surely, your father should be doing that?"

"Oh, no!" she replied. "It has to be the bull!"

+++++++++++

LATER that same day, Martha came close to wrecking a national newspaper's undercover stakeout.

Photographer John Watts was lying flat on his stomach in the boot of his car, his camera focused on 74, Bedwas Villas.

John was patiently waiting to 'snatch' a well-known married Welsh MP, who had spent several hours with a flighty superstore manageress, when he should have been in the Commons.

Having watched the boot-lid moving up and down, Martha went out and tapped on it, and asked, “Would you like a cup of tea, sir?”

John’s unprintable reply was so blunt that 82-year-old Martha came close to breaking the land speed record in her frantic dash home.

+++++++++++

JOE Bevan did so well in his school exams that his mother baked a special cake for his tenth birthday, and put a 20p coin in it.

Joe was enjoying a large slice when the coin became stuck in his throat.

His mother rushed him into the street, where a man picked him up, and punched him hard between the shoulders, and the coin flew out.

“Thank you so much, doctor,” said Mrs. Bevan.

“But I’m not a doctor,” replied the man. “I’m a tax collector!”

+++++++++++

HONEST John Roberts, a deacon at Bethel, boasted that he had never lied to his wife, Lucy.

So when he borrowed a rod to go fishing with best friend Richard Dennis, and came away with nothing, he feared Lucy would laugh at him.

So he dashed to Mickey Salmon’s fish bar, picked out a large trout, and asked Mickey to throw it to him.

And as John grabbed it, he whispered, with a smile, “Now I can honestly tell her that I really did catch it. I’d never lie to Lucy.”

+++++++++++

INFAMOUS burglar, Nick Silver, told the local

underworld of the night he broke into the posh house on the hill, and was moving around in the dark when a voice said, “Jesus is watching you. He’s watching you closely.”

Nick recalled that he crept to a corner, where he found a parrot in a cage, and asked it: “Was it you who warned me that Jesus was watching?”

“Yes, that was me,” said the parrot.

Then Nick asked, “So what is your name?”

“It’s Ebenezer,” replied the parrot.

“What a silly name,” said Nick. “What moron called you that?”

“The same moron that called the bulldog Jesus…”

TOP London psychiatrist Ivor Brain was called to treat indoor games champion Tiddlywinks Williams, who’s not been right since he lost his marbles.

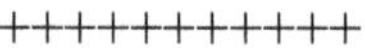

SPINSTER Hilda Griffiths, who never wore make-up, was standing alongside two alabaster mannequins in Marks & Spencer, when the floor manager advised her to move on, as she could end up in the van with the others.

JUNE

Frantic search for missing Molly

AS usual, the third Saturday in June was greeted with great excitement as 140 children and parents stepped aboard three Mike Harris coaches for the annual Sunday school outing to Barry Island.

Every church and chapel was represented on a blazing hot day, and everyone settled down on the beach with their ham-and-egg sandwiches, cream cakes, scones, and gallons of orange juice and lemonade.

It was a jolly scene on a glorious day that was about to plunge into desperate panic.

Little Molly Watkins suddenly vanished on the beach. One minute she was playing happily in the sand alongside Susan, her mum, and then she was gone.

Molly had turned six the previous week, and was wearing a bright yellow swimming costume that Susan had deliberately bought so that Molly could be seen at all times.

Susan ran up and down the crowded beach calling out "Molly! Molly!" but there was no response.

Superintendent Matthews, head of Aber Tidy police, was soon on the scene, together with several uniformed officers, and the search quickly extended beyond the beach into nearby streets and lanes.

A police helicopter hovered above, and the local Lifeboat was launched, in case Molly had wandered into the sea.

Concern soared when Supt. Matthews confidentially told Susan that a dangerous paedophile had escaped from prison, and that undercover police officers were keeping a close watch on his family home, just a mile from where Molly went missing.

Police roadblocks were set up all around the town, and two skilled sniffer dogs joined the search.

Finding no clue on the beach, the dogs were taken to nearby fields and gardens, and eventually ended up at the main car park, where Susan had left her red BMW.

By now an eerie silence had developed among the searchers, as concern for Molly grew bigger and bigger.

And then, when everyone feared the worst, a shout, like a thunderclap, echoed around the car park.

"Found her! Found her!" bellowed an ecstatic police officer, his voice cracking with relief and emotion.

Everyone surged, like a tidal wave, to the beaming officer, who was standing alongside Susan's car, and holding Molly tightly in his arms.

Susan led the charge, and gently took Molly from the officer. Tears cascaded down her face, and there was enormous leaping with joy.

When everything had settled down, Molly explained that she had taken the car key from her mother's handbag, and gone to the car for her bucket and spade in the boot.

But they were so far out of reach that Molly had to climb into the boot, and just as she got to them, the lid came down and trapped her inside.

Then she cried, and cried, and fell into a deep sleep.

Loudest cheer went to Chester, the brilliant sniffer dog, who had cleverly led the searchers to Molly in the boot.

And in a spontaneous show of gratitude, a thrilled Susan ignited everyone with a rousing chorus of "For he's a jolly good Chester!"

+++++++++++

AMBITIOUS drama student Marion Rees became confused when applying for an acting role, and wrote to the boss at Holloway (prison) in North London, instead of Hollywood in America, and landed a leading part in the TV drama Cell Block H.

+++++++++++

ANGRY Tony Jones summoned his two best mates to a meeting at the Castle Hotel.

He told them that he would no longer be taking their advice on his holiday plans.

He recalled that his wife became pregnant during his two-week break in Barcelona three years ago, again while in Florida two years ago, and yet again last year when in New York.

Thumping the table, he said: "This year, she's coming with me!"

+++++++++++

ABER Tidy police charged elastic maker Chris Miller for selling slack, sub-standard knickers to elderly ladies.

Miller apologized for letting them down, but expects a long stretch when his case comes up in court.

+++++++++++

JAKE Proverb was deservedly crowned Cliché champion for his entry…

"Having not slept a wink, it slowly dawned that if life is to be plain sailing, I must never get the wind up; and I must never put my foot down when I don't have a leg to stand on. And when it rains cats and dogs I must remember that every cloud has a silver lining. And at the end of the day, tying them in a knot can be money for old rope..."

The judges also praised runner-up Pamela Harrison "who clearly knew her onions", and recommended that she worked at the pickle factory.

+++++++++++

Council housing department confirmed that chicken farmer Cook-a-doodle-do, had moved up the pecking order!

+++++++++++

NANCY Morris was happily married to Dan, and when their first child arrived she called to see Tom Thomas, the best butcher in Doolally Valley.

Nancy told him that the baby was his, and if he didn't want his wife to know, he'd have to provide free meat every week until it was 16.

Tom was trapped, and couldn't refuse, so for 16 years he filled Nancy's large basket with the best British steaks, thick Danish gammon, succulent pies, and fat chickens.

On the lad's 16th birthday, Nancy told him to call with Tom, and to thank him for everything he'd given them, and to watch his face when he told him that she'd also been having free milk, free fruit and veg, free house insurance, and free petrol for 16 years, as well…

JULY

Doped Duke in Derby farce!

THE Duke of Norfolk entered his brilliant colt Bolt Up to run in the Aber Tidy Derby, and was walking to the paddock to give it a 'good luck' pat when he saw his trainer slip something into its mouth.

"What was that that you just gave him?" asked the Duke.

"No big deal," replied the trainer.

"Here, you have one, and I'll have one."

So they both took a pill, and the Duke went back to his private room to watch the race.

The trainer was then heard telling his jockey: "Hold him up till a furlong out. Then let him go. And if anything passes you, it will either be me or the Duke of Norfolk…"

+++++++++++

TOP jockey Willie Wynne is to face a grilling from Aber Tidy stewards over an incident at the Festival meeting.

A thick mist fell in mid-afternoon, and blotted out all

12 runners in the 3.45 race.

Starter Mark Miller told the jockeys, "All those trying, please move forward."

Six horses advanced to the tape, with the rest staying well back.

Willie Wynne was riding 50-1 outsider, Fingers Crossed, seeking its first win in 26 races.

Willie set off in last place, and after trotting less than 200 yards he pulled the horse up, and waited in the fog until he heard the pack coming up behind him.

Fresh and keen, Fingers Crossed made the short dash to the winning-post ahead of them all, and finished sixth!

Trainer Keith Hardman said: "A big improvement, when you consider that he was so slow in his last race that he finished behind the ambulance."

+++++++++++

EARLIER in the day, a lump of lead fell out of Willie Wynne's weight cloth, and on returning to the scales, the clerk said, "I see you lost three pounds in that race, Mr. Wynne."

"That's nothing, sir," replied the jockey, "I lost a hundred and fifty in the first!"

+++++++++++

APPRENTICE jockeys were required to test their weight before officially stepping on the scales to ride in a race.

When the clerk asked Justin Tyme whether he'd tried, the young rider replied; "Not yet, sir, but we're trying today!"

+++++++++++

AWARD-winning school cleaner Anisa Swales has not been seen since she spilt a bottle of Vanish in the headmaster's study.

The powerful cleaning liquid also spirited away two chairs and a piano.

+++++++++++

FOR six years, frustrated Colin Jones longed to be called into action as a fire officer at Aber Tidy International Airport.

Every day, he ate his corn beef sandwiches, polished the three fire engines, and went home exasperated.

Then, on July 4, the pilot of a German airliner, packed with 350 passengers, radioed that smoke was belching from under both wings, and that he was diverting to Aber Tidy.

All emergency services were put on red alert, and scores of flashing blue lights lit up the airport concourse as police cars, ambulances, and the public fire service arrived from every direction.

It was like a chaotic Hollywood blockbuster scene, crammed with all the drama and tension Colin had yearned six years to see.

But it was his day off, and he missed it all!

"Typical," he grunted, and recalled the day his new car fell off the delivery lorry; his world cruise was cancelled when the liner needed urgent repairs; and his wedding organist was shopping when he should have been playing at the church.

"Anyone like to buy my lottery ticket?" he joked, and carried on eating and polishing…

+++++++++++

BLACKSMITHS Hammer & Tongs sacked apprentice Glyn Lewis because when asked to shoe a shire horse he kept repeating "Shoo! Shoo! Shoo!" and the horse kept going backwards until it reached the mountain road to Caerphilly.

++++++++++++

DAI ‘twp’ Richards went into the Coop and asked to buy the small TV set in the corner.

But the manager rushed out and told Dai that he was not welcome there, and he wouldn’t be served.

So Dai went home, borrowed his wife’s ginger wig, picked up his dark glasses, and went back, and tried again.

But the manager quickly saw through Dai’s disguise, and reminded him that he’d been told he wouldn’t be served.

So Dai went home for a second time, squeezed into his wife’s floral dress, painted his face with her make-up, pulled on a blonde wig, and went back, wobbling precariously on a pair of high heels.

He staggered into the Coop, entirely altered his voice, and asked to buy the small TV-set in the corner.

Yet again the manager saw him, and ordered him to leave, so Dai asked: “How did you know it was me?”

“Easy,” said the manager, “because it’s a microwave!”

++++++++++++

ABER Tidy’s top vet Paddy O’Connor struggled through the trickiest month of his 15-year career.

He treated a giraffe for a sore throat, a centipede with bunions, a crocodile with toothache, a cockerel with chickenpox, and made a trunk call for an elephant.

AUGUST

Baby boom for desperate Maggie!

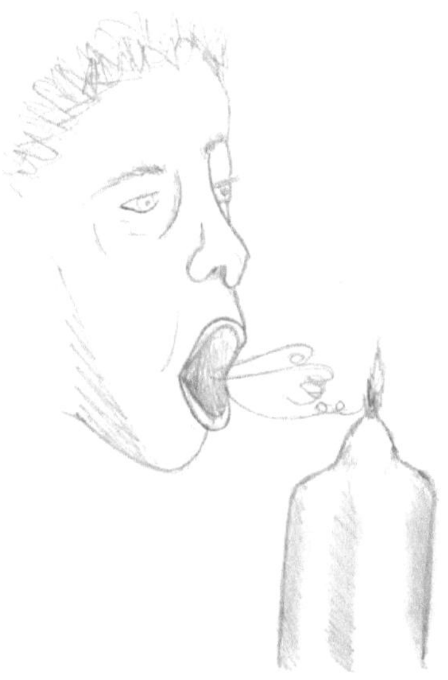

WHEN Maggie Morris met Father Brown in Goose Road five years ago, she politely asked him to pray for her to have a baby.

Father Brown said he would do more than just pray for Maggie, adding that he was going to Rome the following week, and that he would light a candle for her in the Vatican.

Five years went by before they again met by chance in Aber Tidy country park.

Maggie was pushing a pram with two small babies inside, and a smiling Father Brown said, "I see you've done well."

Maggie chuckled, and replied, "I've also got Dylan and Mary at school, and Dafydd is with my mother…"

"Great," said Father Brown. "And where is your

husband?"

"Oh, he's in Rome, blowing out the candle!"

+++++++++++

CRICKET club chairman Morley Howell announced that fast bowler Howard Morgan's problem with 'no balls' was a well-known cricket term, and that everything was working well with him physically.

Morley went on to assure everyone that Aber Tidy cricketers did not have 'square legs' or a 'short third man,' or 'bowl maidens over'. It was all cricket terminology.

+++++++++++

MORTON Evans, popular owner of Valley Taxis, picked up a Japanese tourist at Heathrow, who was on his way to Aber Tidy Festival Week.

All along the M4, the tourist kept repeating, "Suzuki GP motor-cycle very fast. Made in Japan. Honda F1 engine, very fast. Made in Japan."

When they reached The Bell hotel, Morton said, "That will be £130.50, please."

"Wow!" said the tourist, "You very expensive."

Pointing to the meter, Morton replied, "That very fast. Made in Japan."

+++++++++++

Doolally Valley's favourite fortune-teller Megan Thomas cleverly masterminded a young couple's future with the help of her crystal-ball.

Meg had been secretly meeting bank clerk Sarah Thorp, who had taken a fancy to interior decorator Adrian Adams, but feared getting the brush off if she made the first move.

So Sarah and Meg plotted to find out how Adrian felt about her.

Sarah had made it plain that he was the Adams apple of

her eye, and persuaded him to visit Meg for a private reading in her tent in Festival Week.

Outside the tent was a large poster, inviting everyone to 'STEP INSIDE AND LET MYSTIC MEG REVEAL YOUR FUTURE'.

Meg asked Adrian to hold her hand, close his eyes, and relax, while she looked into the crystal-ball.

Very quickly, and in a husky voice, she said, "There's something strong coming through about your personal life.

"I see a lovely young lady. It's someone you know. I see a wonderful future for you both together.

"Can you think of who that might be?"

Adrian smiled, and nodded. He looked very pleased.

"Thank you," he said, paid his £10, and left, with a definite skip in his step.

He was so impressed that he stopped at the pawnshop on his way home, hoping to buy a crystal-ball to help with his lottery numbers.

It certainly was his lucky day, as there were two for sale, and he bought them both.

Now, exactly 12 months later, Sarah and Adrian were joyously married, and Meg was a special top-table guest.

As the speeches closed, Sarah suddenly stood up, and said, "Meg, I thank you so much for bringing us together.

"We are very happy, and having a great time playing with his crystal-balls."

The laughter went on late into the night!

+++++++++++

FARMER Mel Bridges built a large swimming pool in a field behind the barn for his grandchildren to play in.

When he returned home after two weeks on holiday, he could hear high pitched voices and giggling coming from the pool.

So Mel picked up a big black bucket and headed towards the pool, and as he turned the corner, he could see the Aber Tidy football team, and their partners, frolicking in the shallow end.

Mel's grandchildren were expected soon, so he wanted the pool cleared for them to go straight in.

But team captain, Alfie Hughes, called out, "You go away, we're here all day. Go away!"

Mel walked up to Alfie and, tapping the bucket on his shoulder, he said, "Please yourself, mate, I'm only here to feed the barracuda in the deep end…"

There was a mighty splash…

+++++++++++

INFAMOUS James twins, Sid and Jesse, were kept in a cell overnight after being arrested trying to seize an ostrich at the zoo.

They had heard of a hostage demand of two million dollars in the United States, and thought they'd cash in. Idiots!

+++++++++++

DAI 'Twp' Richards formed a powerful vigilante group, which included Lord Rimmer, to storm the bank with cutting equipment once he heard that the manager was meeting a number of Italian 'businessmen' and would be tied up. He feared the Mafia.

+++++++++++

SEPTEMBER

Dodgy Freddie's dogs get a splash of colour

SHADY greyhound trainer Freddie Baker travelled all over the UK to land prizes and big bets.

Freddie always ran his dogs on unlicensed tracks, where no checks were made on their identity.

Slippery Freddie took full advantage, and cheated his way to stacks of money until an unexpected cloudburst literally washed away his lucrative ruse.

Freddie's greyhound was crossing the winning line when the rain teemed down.

Suddenly, a mixture of many colours could be seen running along the dog's back, and down his face and legs.

Freddie frantically grabbed the greyhound, bundled it onto the back seat, and disappeared over the hill at high speed.

The game was up. Freddie had been painting two very fast greyhounds with dots and flashes before races to conceal their identity, and changing their names every time they ran.

Freddie had no choice but to quit dog racing, and he promptly took up interior decorating, mainly not to waste all the paint he had left over in the shed.

+++++++++++

WHEN William Shakespeare, who lives with his family in Barry John Close, called at the Royal Oak pub, the barman said: "You can't come in here, you're bard!"

+++++++++++

SISTER Anna and Sister Mary were fuming when a boy racer, and his noisy mates, nearly crashed into them at the Aber Tidy roundabout.

Sister Anna told Sister Mary, who was driving, "Go on, show them your cross!"

Sister Mary thought she meant to show them she was angry, so she rolled down the window, and unleashed such a volley of abuse that Sister Anna cringed, and prayed for her.

Later, when everything was back to normal, Sister Anna joked, "We're nuns, so no bad habits!"

+++++++++++

TOP prize at Aber Tidy's annual vegetable show went to a Swede from Stockholm.

+++++++++++

CARPENTER Colin Wood, who has fitted 134 doors in the past ten years, was finally nominated for the No-bell Prize!

+++++++++++

WHEN lorry owner Will Briggs was unable to collect three East African monkeys that had arrived at Southampton Docks, a willing Dai 'twp' Richards offered to step in for him.

Will told Dai: "These monkeys are to go to Chester Zoo, and here's £100 to fill the tank."

So Dai set off early, but when the lorry came back in the evening, the monkeys were still on it.

Shocked, and puzzled, Will rushed out, and said: "I told you to take them to Chester Zoo, so what happened?"

Dai replied: "Well, as I had money left over after filling the tank, I took them to Alton Towers, instead!"

+++++++++++

CHURCH choir leader Hilda Harris changed her tune, and resigned, and opened a massage parlour.

She named it Hilda's Hotpot, and told shocked choristers: "I feel my nimble fingers can do a lot better than thump an old piano with dodgy keys."

Husband Rhys, and 'Oddjob' Lewis, said they were happy in Petra's Steamy Parlour, and would keep going there.

Bass chorister Alun 'Bottom C' promised to pop in when the 'dragon' was on holiday, or "blood would cascade."

+++++++++++

PEGGY Potts took Bruno, her overweight Boxer, to the vet when he couldn't shake off a runny nose.

Paddy O'Connor examined him closely, and said, "I'm sorry, but I'll have to put him down."

"What!" exclaimed Peggy. "Put him down with just a runny nose?"

"Oh, no," grinned Paddy, "he's just got a bit heavy to hold."

OCTOBER

Top dogs run away with 'hero' awards!

TWO remarkable dogs won the valley's annual life-saving award. One was a psychic terrier named Rossi.

The other was 'sniffer' Chester, who produced a classic piece of canine detective work to find missing Molly in her mum's car boot.

Rossi's alarm call at Gill Wilson's beautiful Rose Cottage was a prodigious award-winning performance.

In a packed town hall, mayor Martin Evans, praised Chester's "fantastic snout," and called on Emili and Marco to recall Rossi's crucial cry for help.

Emili said: "Rose Cottage stands alongside the public

path to Aber Tidy park. We've walked it many times, and Rossi knows it well.

"On this particular day, we'd let Rossi off the lead just as we approached the cottage, and he raced away to the backdoor, where Gill always had something nice for him.

"Only this time, there was no sign of Gill, and Rossi immediately sensed something was wrong, and pushed his body against the door, which swung open, and he darted inside.

"He barked so loudly, they probably heard him in Cwmscoot, over the mountain in the next valley.

"Marco and I rushed in, and found Gill flat out, unconscious, on the kitchen floor. She'd clearly tripped over the dirty washing basket, and slammed her head against the fridge."

Emili and Marco promptly rang for an emergency ambulance, fed Rossi the biscuits Gill had prepared for him, and slipped a pillow under her head, as she slowly woke up.

It took ten days for Gill to recover in Aber Tidy General, where doctors said any further delay would have put her life in danger.

"So Rossi's a hero," crowed Emili, and brought him on stage to accept the applause.

It also reminded everyone that Aber Tidy, like any other town, had very serious moments, and that it wasn't always fun and games.

+++++++++++

GOLF icon Alan Wedge revealed that he always wore two pairs of socks in tournaments in case he had a hole in one, which had not happened in 42 years!

+++++++++++

POLICE officers surrounded The Bell after a ding-dong between two inebriated customers, and one was heard to say, “I could murder one of those Foster’s!”

+++++++++++

HEATHER Davies finally passed her driving test at the 15th attempt, and on her 83rd birthday.

To get there, she had spent more than £3,000 for 200 lessons, damaged three driving school cars, knocked down a lamppost, and caused two instructors to retire early.

Heather’s tortured examiner went straight back to rehab, where the owner later stated that he had started to turn the corner…

+++++++++++

KATHY Seymour was crowned Football Fan of the Year at a special ceremony in a packed town hall.

It came as no surprise, as the hugely likeable Chelsea supporter had painted her whole house, inside and outside, in the club’s well-known blue, and proudly renamed it Stamford Bridge 2.

Judges visited the unique property in Bluebell Lane, and noted that Kathy…

- Had replaced a number of doors with squeaky Chelsea turnstiles, and painted them blue.
- Drove a blue Civic saloon from the Honda Valley, registration CHE 1SE.
- Ate a Chelsea bun at ten every morning, along with a cup of tea and blue-top milk.
- Covered every wall with club scarves, signed shirts, autographed portraits of players, set in blue frames, and even jockstraps dyed blue that had been worn by the club’s international stars.

To a recording of Blue Moon, a smiling Kathy strode on stage, her hair blue, dressed entirely in blue, and wearing spectacles in large blue frames, made famous by Dame Edna.

While accepting the award – a large, blue inscribed dinner plate - from Aber Tidy FC president, Peter Thomas, a rabid Swansea City fan, she said: "From the bottom of my heart, I thank everyone who has supported me and Chelsea.

"And to those who wonder whether I sleep in blue, there is just one person here tonight who knows the answer to that, but the secret is safe with me, Dewi…"

At this point, Dewi Griffiths leapt to his feet and dashed to the door, closely followed by his wife, Hilda, wildly waving an umbrella high above her head, and screaming expletives at him.

The air was blue!

+++++++++++

ON a steaming hot afternoon, fanatical Welsh speaker Alun-ap-Hazard was walking along a bank high above the Aber River when he saw a man bending down scooping water into his mouth to quench his thirst.

Alun panicked, as he knew that toxic chemicals from the nearby plastics factory were entering the river at that exact spot.

So he urgently shouted down to the man in Welsh, warning him not to put a single drop of the contaminated water to his lips.

The man stood up, and called back, "Is there a problem? I didn't understand a word of what you said."

Alun responded: "You an Englishman drinking our wonderful Welsh water. Enjoy it. Drink as much as you can!"

+++++++++++

A stranger strolled into the Red Lion pub, and the barman said, "What would you like, sir?"

"A scotch and a little water would do fine, thank you,"

he replied.

The barman handed him the drink, and said, “That will be £1.90, please, sir.”

“Oh, no,” said the stranger. “You asked me what I’d like to drink. Isn’t that right?” he asked a man sitting at the bar, who was a solicitor.

Pink with rage, the barman ranted: “Drink it down, and never set foot in this place again.”

So the stranger drank the Scotch and left, but he was back in less than an hour.

As he walked through the door, the barman called out: “I thought I told you never to set foot in this place again!”

“But I’ve never been in this place before,” pleaded the stranger.

“Well, in that case you must have a double,” conceded the barman.

“Oh, thank you very much,” said the stranger, “ and I’ll have one for my solicitor friend, as well...”

NOVEMBER

Dai 'Twp' in pilot's licence drama

ABER Tidy came to a full stop at 11.00 a.m. on the 11th when Dai 'twp' Richards took his pilot's test.

A loudspeaker was fitted to a large white van parked outside the town hall, which enabled everyone within 50 yards to hear Dai answering questions from an examiner in the control tower.

When asked where he was, Dai answered, "I'm in the front by the window."

And when asked to give his height, he replied, "I'm exactly five feet, ten."

Then when quizzed about what he knew of the landing, Dai responded, "It's at the top of the stairs."

It was Dai's first time in the air, as all his training had been done on a simulator.

Panic spread on the ground when the plane suddenly emerged from behind a cloud, and Dai could be seen eating a sandwich in one hand, while waving furiously with the other.

A loud knocking noise could also be heard coming from the aircraft.

A retired BA pilot, who was standing in the crowd, identified it as the examiner's knees banging together, like a pair of castanets, as Dai prepared to bring the plane down.

Women and children were given priority in a sudden dash for safety.

Dai could now be seen with both hands wrapped around a large bottle of ginger-beer, his favourite day-time drink.

The examiner then frantically lunged forward to grab the controls, and the plane swayed from side to side, before bouncing along the runway like a giant kangaroo.

Dai was down and, miraculously, no-one was hurt, though a long queue had formed outside the pharmacy for the strongest Valium to calm tattered nerves.

Bookies also rushed to take bets on whether Dai had done enough to pass.

Pompously sticking his chest out, Dai strode into the examiner's office, and in just ten minutes he emerged, waving a brown 'pass' certificate, and shouting, "I'm a pilot! I'm a pilot!"

A pale, trembling examiner then appeared, and sheepishly confirmed, "Yes, he's passed. I just couldn't go through all that again!

"And the best of luck to everyone who has to fly with him!"

Staring at the ground, the exhausted examiner walked slowly back to his office, threw himself into a chair, sank a double-Scotch, booked a month in Barbados, and resigned…

+++++++++++

PETE Roberts was so desperate for a job that he became a postman without disclosing he was a chronic dyslexic.

Which explained why Post Office bosses were baffled when a parcel of high quality knickers meant for Winnie Brown ended up with Willie Broom.

Then letters for George Finch went to Georgina Fish, and Michael Bell's mail was ending up with Michele Ball, and Steve Smith's with Eve Sims, as well as many more going to the wrong people.

Fortunately for the Post Office, problem Pete quit after a month, and applied to join the BBC as a TV newsreader.

+++++++++++

PRANKSTERS Joe King and Olly Legpull are facing a long term in jail for deliberately wasting police time in a 'double murder' investigation.

An alleged dog walker – later believed to be King – reported seeing two male bodies with holes in the head, lying alongside each other in Aber Tidy park.

It was 6.30 a.m. when the phone call came into the police station, appropriately taken by Dawn, whose elder sister, Dusk, worked on the evening shift.

Supt. Matthews immediately engaged two police helicopters, and rushed to the park to head the inquiry, followed by ten officers crammed in a police van.

Firmly in charge, Supt. Matthews instructed his officers to remain 50 yards from the prostrate bodies until the forensic team had arrived, and given the 'all clear' to go forward.

Using his powerful binoculars, Supt. Matthews could clearly see a hole in each forehead, directly above the nose, and large patches of what appeared to be blood spread across the face.

While the officers patiently waited for the forensic team, the Marks & Spencer store manager was entering the building, right opposite the police station.

Within seconds, he could see that there had been an overnight raid. Two alabaster mannequins were missing, along with a couple of dinner suits, two white shirts, bow ties, and black shoes.

He went straight to the police station, but was met with a closed door, as every officer was out, seeking clues for what seemed a horrific double murder.

Supt. Matthews, the first top cop to rule out suicide in the Shergar case, was asked if this could be a serial killer, and he cautiously replied: “Do you have a particular cereal in mind?”

Ten forensic experts finally arrived, all dressed in long, white hooded cloaks, and mumbling in a strange language, which reminded Supt. Matthews of the Bards at the National Eisteddfod.

Supt. Matthews then went forward to inspect the ‘crime scene’, surrounded with enough blue-and-white security tape to bind a herd of elephants.

As he approached the supposed murder victims, Supt. Matthews became seriously agitated, and began muttering expletives under his breath. He was a proverbial time-bomb about to explode.

He could now see that the two so-called bodies were alabaster mannequins, smartly dressed in M & S dinner suits, and that the holes in the head had been drilled, and bright red paint splashed around them to look like blood.

“They’ve stuffed me!” stormed Supt. Matthews, confident that deadly duo Joe King and Olly Legpull had made a fool of him.

Waving his arms in anger, he called off the search, sent the helicopters back to base, and escorted the forensic team to their van.

Joe King and Olly Legpull were caught on CCTV boarding a ferry to Calais, so Supt. Matthews promptly contacted Interpol’s dynamic Agent Fageant, who always gets her man…

FOR once, 325 pupils were sitting in total silence in the primary school’s assembly hall, respectfully waiting for the world’s most popular headmaster, John Walters, to walk on stage.

It was a deeply sad day, as Mr. Walters was about to

deliver his retirement speech after 30 years' teaching at the school.

Cheers, and oceans of tears, greeted their hero, as he waved his white handkerchief, Pavarotti style, and smiled gently behind his thick, grey beard.

He praised the pupils, saluted his teaching colleagues, thanked the kitchen staff, and recalled the morning that a heavy cold forced the school's top scorer to drop out of an important football match, which left them without a centre-forward.

Mr. Walters recalled: "So I went to every classroom, and eventually pointed to Jasper Thomas, and said, "'Right, you're in the team. You're not much good, but you're in…'

"And he scored two brilliant goals and won the match for us. It was the start of a huge career.

"You'll know that Jasper is now the leading scorer with a top Spanish football team, and all because he played…"

Suddenly, a deafening "Wow!" erupted in the hall, as Jasper came out from behind the curtains, smartly dressed in his club's famous red jersey.

Mr. Walters welcomed him warmly, and recounted many amusing school moments in which he took part.

As the children cheered, and Jasper turned to leave, he was passed by deputy head, Austin Keep, who was carrying a clock to present to Mr. Walters as the customary 'thank you' retirement gift.

After a torrent of compliments about Mr. Walters' inspiration and "goodness", Mr. Keep was literally handing over the clock when Mr. Walters fumbled it, and it crashed to the floor.

The children laughed and laughed. Some might still be laughing today. It was that funny.

Mr. Walters hung his head low. It was a pantomime scene that had come a few weeks early.

Very gradually Mr. Walters pulled himself together and apologized, and said that he no longer had plans to be a music hall juggler!

But it had all been brilliantly staged to give the children, many of them from poor homes, where laughs were rare, a real chance to let rip, like they'd never done before.

Fewer than ten people knew that the clock Mr. Walters dropped was his own, and had been covered in dust in his loft for more than ten years.

The brand new 'presentation' one was safely wrapped in a box in the boot of his car.

Right to the end, John Walters was the master of inspirational magic.

+++++++++++

TWO council clerks were recovering in hospital after handling a powerful repellant that they had put down when told they had a mole in the office.

+++++++++++

REV. Bryn Williams was taking his dog, Betsy, for a walk when he met handyman Ted Graham, working hard on rebuilding an old farmhouse that he had recently bought.

It was a mammoth mess, with timber and bricks piled high, overgrown bushes blocking paths, and a leaking roof with several slates missing.

"A daunting task," said Rev. Williams, "but I'm sure God will help you put it right."

About eight months later, Rev. Williams was again passing the farmhouse with Betsy when he stopped in shock, and admiration, as he saw the building had been beautifully completed.

Rev. Williams called out to Ted, "You and God have done a fantastic job together."

"A great deal better than what he did on his own," snapped Ted.

+++++++++++

MANDY Davies saved a lot of money by growing her own vegetables on the council allotment.

Then one morning, she found that all the earth had gone.

Baffled and confused, she rang her husband and said, "Geoffrey, I've completely lost the plot!"

He showed no surprise, as he'd seen the signs for sometime.

+++++++++++

FERRET breeder Damien Brierley revealed that he had stopped smoking, drinking, watching TV, eating pies, fries, and burghers--- and that it was the worst 20 minutes of his life…

+++++++++++

STEVE Thomas was rated the nicest guy on the planet, and could almost touch one from his top flat, 30 storeys high, in Skyscraper Tower.

The only communal telephone was on the ground floor, and when it rang at 3.30 one morning, Steve hopped out of bed, and hurried down 42 concrete steps to answer it.

"Is that Aber Tidy two, two, three, three?" asked a quiet voice.

"No. Sorry, mate. This is Aber Tidy double two, double three."

"Very sorry to bother you," apologized the caller. "No trouble," said Steve, "I had to come down, the phone was ringing."

DECEMBER

Guard dogs 'operate' at hospital!

IN a public statement, the head of Aber Tidy General Hospital told patients that the notice at the main gate 'Guard dogs operate here' should not be taken literally.

He said the dogs had not been trained to carry out operations, though thy had been known to take blood…

+++++++++++

CHARITY worker Ianto Bevan saved every spare coin to buy Christmas gifts for his family.

Then a Revenue inspector called to work out what he owed them.

After an hour, the inspector said, "We are all helping the country with our taxes, so try paying them with a smile."

"Oh, thank you very much," said Ianto. "For a moment, I thought you were going to ask for money."

+++++++++++

MANSEL Thomas ended the year in the same way that he began it, with yet another controversial statement.

The feisty council leader began the Festive season by slating President Trump for not even responding to an invitation to switch on the Christmas lights, and was "surprised" Real Madrid had turned down the chance to challenge Aber Tidy FC on Boxing Day.

Councillor Thomas said, "Who do these people think they are? They seem to regard us as crackpots because we live here in Aber Tidy, the international capital of wit and wisdom.

"I offered to pay for the President to stay in the best room at the Castle Hotel, which has a great view of our brand new pickle factory, but even that didn't tempt him.

"And the YMCA were happy to waive their dormitory fee for the Real Madrid squad, and even provide hot-water bottles in Real colours."

With time on his hands, watch-repairer Ianto Bremner agreed to switch on the lights in place of the President, and Doolally Rangers welcomed the chance to play in place of Real.

+++++++++++

SUPT. Matthews stressed that the notice outside the police station 'Man Wanted for Stealing Christmas Trees' was not an advertisement.

And he urged everyone to stop sending pictures of their tree-felling equipment.

+++++++++++

DAI 'twp' Richards fell 30 feet down a shaft at the disused Aber Tidy coal mine, and when work-mate Ianto Howgate asked if he had broken anything, Dai shouted back, "Don't be daft, boyo, there's nothing down here to break!"

+++++++++++

BOOKIE Ben Wright put his wife, Sally, up for sale in The Gazette's main motoring page.

He priced her at £50 or nearest offer. Part-exchange would also be considered, provided it was young, and attractive.

Ben's hilarious advert said: "For sale, second-hand wife; 1956 model; good condition, but slow to start in the morning. £50 or nearest. Would consider part-exchange for younger model.

"Lots left on the clock; good chassis; no rust. "

One frugal Scot would only go to £40, and wanted a year's warranty "on all vital parts."

When Gazette reporter Ivor Scoop called to interview Sally, she went straight into overdrive, and locked herself in the garage.

A calmer Ben said: "When she saw it in The Gazette, she blew a gasket. She was steaming.

"But it was nothing that a bit of charm, box of chocolates, and a bunch of red roses couldn't put right.

"She eventually saw the funny side of it, which was great, as I didn't get one decent offer. So I'm still left with a slow, tired old banger.

"But don't dare tell her that or you'll be writing my obit."

+++++++++++

MY unforgettable 12 months in Aber Tidy ended on December 20, after I'd sung most of my favourite carols around the huge Christmas tree in the town square.

Then I was made to feel like royalty with a front-row seat at the junior school nativity play, which was brilliant.

My colossal experience was over. It was time to go home.

I had reveled in the company of some fantastic people, and witnessed exciting incidents that I could never have imagined.

Throughout my time in Aber Tidy, I stayed with the

incomparable Martha Bowen, a compulsive nosey-parker, whose curtains had frayed from all the pulling and peeping that she had done.

What she told me in confidence would shock and shame scores of big wigs all over the valley.

She was a wonderful raconteur, and a real Mary Berry in the kitchen.

Mansel Thomas, John Walters, Dai 'twp' Richards, 'Butterfingers Jenkins', and even Ted Curtis, who did so much to educate schoolchildren at Aber Tidy rainforest, came out to wave me goodbye.

I have promised to go back, and I'm already looking forward to it…

End

www.ingramcontent.com/pod-product-compliance
Ingram Content Group UK Ltd.
Pitfield, Milton Keynes, MK11 3LW, UK
UKHW042000190726
13854UKWH00005B/2087

9 781789 552232